THREADING THE SPACE NEEDLE

BY SEAN PETRIE
ILLUSTRATED BY CARL PEARCE

Book design by Jake Slavik
Illustrations by Carl Pearce

Photographs ©: Shutterstock Images, 67; Gene Blevins/Zuma Press/Newscom, 68

Published in the United States by Jolly Fish Press, an imprint of North Star Editions, Inc.

First Edition
First Printing, 2021

Library of Congress Cataloging-in-Publication Data (pending)
978-1-63163-559-5 (paperback)
978-1-63163-558-8 (hardcover)

Jolly Fish Press
North Star Editions, Inc.
2297 Waters Drive
Mendota Heights, MN 55120
www.jollyfishpress.com

Printed in the United States of America

TABLE OF CONTENTS

CHAPTER 1

Jett Ryder stood beneath the dizzyingly tall tower and craned his neck upward.

"Just looking at it, I feel like I'm flying," he said.

He was at the base of the Seattle Space Needle with his best friend, Mika Moore. It was a clear summer day, and they were in line for the elevator to the top. Above them, the Needle's massive sides sloped gracefully upward, like three giant ladders propped together, pointing to the sky.

"I love how it doesn't compete with nature," said Mika. "It blends with it."

Halfway up the Needle, a seagull darted through one of the wide, sky-filled openings in its support beams. The gull held its wings out, floating on the breeze.

"That would be so cool to soar like that," said Jett.

"Soaring?" asked Jett's dad. "Did someone say soaring?"

Jett's parents had joined them in line, along with Mika's mom. Both families lived close to Seattle and were on a day trip to the city.

"Is soaring part of your next stunt?" asked his dad, rubbing his hands together excitedly.

Jett was the world's most famous motocross

daredevil. And at twelve years old, he was also the youngest.

"He just finished the last one," said his mom. "Let him take a break."

A seagull flew past, letting out a *squawk squawk!*

"The gulls agree," said Mika's mom.

They all laughed.

"Actually," his dad said, "I happen to speak seagull, and I'm certain it was saying, *What's next, Jett? What's next?*"

Jett grinned. His dad could charm a sea slug. He was also Jett's co-manager.

"I'm totally ready for the next stunt," Jett said.

"For something big . . ." High above, the Needle's swooping sides seemed to point not just to the sky and space, but to the future. "Something as big as the Needle!"

"Now you're talking!" said his dad.

They all boarded the elevator and were whisked upward. When the doors opened at the top, Jett and Mika rushed to the edge of the observation deck.

Far below, the green-blue water of the bay stretched in nearly all directions, dotted by tiny whitecaps and huge cargo ships. To the southeast, the city skyline rippled beneath them. All of it was set against a backdrop of towering mountains. A light

breeze blew, and Jett smelled the sea salt of the
ocean, mixed with the evergreen trees that lined
Seattle's hills.

"Best view in the city," said Mika.

"In the world," said Jett.

"They passed a law to protect it," said Mika's mom.
She was an attorney and responsible for handling all

the paperwork for Jett's stunts. "Everything around the Needle has to be a lot shorter. That keeps the view up here clear. And it lets people on the ground see the Needle from almost anywhere in the city."

"Which means if we jumped it," said Jett's dad, "they could see the stunt for miles!"

"Our son is not jumping his motocross bike over the Space Needle," said his mom. "That's not even close to safe." She was Jett's other co-manager. His dad was the king of promotion. His mom was the queen of practicality.

"It's also impossible," said Mika.

If anyone knew, it would be Mika. Not only was

she Jett's best friend, but Mika Moore was also a twelve-year-old engineering whiz. She and her crew designed all his stunts.

"The Needle is more than six hundred feet high," Mika explained. "That's about five hundred feet out of range. Even for Jett Ryder."

There was a loud gasp behind them. "You're Jett Ryder?"

Jett turned to see a little boy, much younger than him, standing with his father. The boy was gaping up at him in awe. Jett's face turned hotter than his engine during a stunt. People didn't usually recognize him without his stunt outfit on.

"He is!" boomed Jett's dad. "Jett Ryder, in the flesh!"

The boy's eyes widened. "Did you really leap over Tesla coils at Niagara Falls?"

"I did," said Jett.

"That is soooooo cool," said the boy.

The boy's father pulled him closer. "It's also very dangerous," he said. "Especially for someone so young."

"I totally agree," Jett said to him quickly. "That's why my motto is 'Practice till Perfect.' I never perform a stunt unless I'm absolutely sure that I'm able to do it safely."

"If it's too risky," added Jett's mom, "I won't let him do it."

"Me neither," said Mika.

"Well, that's good to hear," said the boy's father.

"You make it look so easy!" the boy said to Jett. "You just sail off a ramp and *whoosh!*" The boy made a motion like a rocket taking off.

"It's not easy," Jett said. "It's taken me years and years of practice. And lots of bruises and cuts and even broken bones. It's a lot of hard work and hard wrecks."

"But . . . do you like it?" the boy asked.

"Once you put in the time and effort, it's amazing."

The boy grinned. "I can't wait for your next jump! What will it be?"

One of Jett's favorite things about doing stunts was how excited people got about them. How it gave them something to root for.

"I'm not sure," Jett said. Then he got a flash of inspiration. "But we'll do it here."

The boy's eyes sparkled. "The Space Needle is the coolest," he said.

"It is," agreed Jett. Now he just had to find a stunt to match it.

CHAPTER 2

On the way back down, the elevator stopped at the Space Needle's lower observation area. It was called the Skyline Level.

Even though it was closer to the ground, the Skyline still offered a sweeping view. In the plaza below, crowds of tourists wandered among museums and sculptures. Families played in wide grassy parks. There was even a monorail.

"This whole place is so awesome," said Jett.

"They built all of it for the World's Fair," said his mom. "Not just the Needle. I forget exactly when."

"It was 1962," said Mika. In addition to being a mechanics genius, she was a major history buff.

"Imagine it," said Jett's dad, with a faraway, dreamy look. He pointed. "Down there, an exhibit on the fastest cars, planes, and rockets!" He pointed again. "There, a hall filled with the newest gadgets and gizmos! And in the shining center, the Needle!"

"Was it really like that?" Jett asked his mom. Sometimes his dad could get carried away.

His mom nodded. "All of the fairs were meant to thrill the world."

"There was more than one?" Jett asked.

"Lots of big cities had a world's fair," answered

Mika. "London was first in the 1800s. But they don't really do them anymore. Not like back then."

Jett's dad spread his arms wide. "We need grand shows like that, to remind us to keep moving forward. To never stay still!"

"Never stay still," repeated Jett. "I like that."

He stepped up to a window and imagined what a spectacle the event must have been. The World's Fair spread out below. The greatest innovators in the world showing off their most amazing inventions. Never staying still.

"I could do a jump down there," Jett said.

"What kind of jump?" asked his dad.

Mika thought for a moment. "You could leap straight up. Break the vertical world record."

"How high would that be?" asked Jett's mom.

"A little over a hundred feet," Mika answered. "That's about how high we are right now. People could watch from here." She pointed to the Skyline's windows.

"We could call it the *Skyline Soar*!" Jett said. He looked to his dad, who seemed less enthusiastic.

"I like the name," Jett's dad said, "but the stunt lacks oomph! You could do that jump beside any building with windows. We need something you could only do here, at the Needle."

Jett sighed. His dad was right. The *Skyline Soar* wasn't quite good enough.

Jett kick-started his bike to life. The noisy two-stroke engine vibrated his whole body. He twisted the throttle and sped across the dirt. It was time for a ride.

With the money from his first few stunts, Jett's parents had rented a practice field outside the city. Mika and her team had fixed it up with a motocross dirt track full of turns and bumps, along with Jett's favorite part: straightaways for pure speed. And jumps.

He shifted gears almost by instinct, racing toward a steep jump. He'd come up with a great idea for the Needle stunt, but he needed to warm up first. He hit the familiar curve of the jump face and shot straight up.

There was nothing like it—the feeling of soaring through sky. For a fraction of a second, Jett *was* a jet. His bike was a sleek flying machine.

His parents and Mika were far below, at the edge of the field. But Jett was careful not to look at them. "You go where your eyes go" was one of the main rules of riding, and Jett didn't want to go downward. Not yet.

He imagined he was a seagull darting through the air. He pictured the clouds laughing with joy as he sailed past them. He pictured himself rocketing six hundred feet to the very top of the Needle, with all of Seattle watching.

Jett let out a wild *whoop!* as he let gravity take over, pulling him on a steady arc back toward the earth. He picked a landing spot on the downside of a hill and focused, willing his bike and body to work as one. He put his front tire down first, matching the downward angle of the hill. Then his back tire landed, and he zoomed across the field toward Mika and his parents.

Jett's heart was revving as fast as his engine. Now he was ready to try the new stunt!

In a large, flat area, Mika's team had built a circular plywood track. Jett dismounted his bike nearby and propped it up with the kickstand.

"Jett, this idea is brilliant!" said his dad.

"It is," agreed his mom. "But it's also a dangerous jump. So, let's make sure you're prepared. Mika, can you walk us through it?"

"Of course." Mika pointed to the circular track. "This is the same size across as the Needle's top deck. Jett will ride halfway around, then do a jump." She pointed to a ramp on the far side that curved back toward them. "He'll leap up and in, going over the Needle."

Jett nodded. "We'll call it *Topping the Needle*!"

His dad clapped his hands. "Excellent!"

"How will he land?" asked Jett's mom.

"After Jett clears the Needle," said Mika, "he'll land on the track on the other side and keep riding in a circle. He'll need to touch down at just the right speed and angle. It's risky, but we'll have a safety fence all around the edge."

Jett's mom nodded. "Thank you, Mika. All right— let's see this leap in action!"

Jett got on his bike and did the stunt, just like Mika had described. But he overshot the jump and went about thirty feet past the circular track. He landed safely on the dirt, then turned around and rode back.

Mika looked ill.

"What's wrong?" Jett asked her.

"If you had done that for real, you would have gone over the safety fence."

Jett swallowed. That meant he would have fallen off the side of the Needle.

"No problem!" said Jett's dad. "You can wear a parachute!"

"You've got to be kidding me," Jett's mom said. "No, no, and no. Six hundred feet of no. Imagine if the parachute didn't open?"

They were all silent, even Jett's dad. Jett knew his stunt idea wouldn't work. But now he had nothing. He thought of that boy, so excited to see him do a jump at the Needle. Jett kicked a pebble across the dirt.

"Jett Ryder," his mom said. "No moping allowed. Get back on that bike." She put her hands on her hips. "And let's race."

Jett looked up. "Really?"

Before he was born, Jett's mom had been a motocross champion. She was the one who had gotten him into riding, almost as soon as he could walk. But she never raced anymore. Jett couldn't remember the last time he'd seen her on a bike.

His mom smiled. "It's been a while, but I bet it'll come back." She turned to Mika. "Do we still have my old bike and gear in the shed?"

"We do. Just give me a few minutes to get the bike tuned up and ready."

Jett felt a surge of excitement. His mom really was going to ride again. Against him!

His dad clapped his hands. "Ryder versus Ryder! Now *this* will be a race!"

CHAPTER 3

Jett flew across the dirt track. His mom rode right

beside him. It had taken a bit to get her old bike

working again, but now it was streaking at full speed.

Both of their engines let out delightful *braaap!* sounds.

There was a sharp turn ahead. Somehow his mom

outmaneuvered him and reached it first. She swung

her leg out for balance, then hit the throttle, spraying

Jett with a rooster tail of dirt. He could almost hear

her laughing.

They sped across a short straightaway toward

a set of whoops. Jett caught up, and they were side

by side. His body shook and shuddered as he rode the series of small bumps in the hard dirt. He let out his own *whoop!* as he bounced across. But his mom had done a wheelie at the start to sail over the first few bumps. Now she was ahead of him, skimming the whoops with ease. She was gliding along, barely touching the top of each.

But there was still one thing left to finish the race: the jump.

Maybe his mom was better at turns and whoops, but Jett owned jumping.

As they zoomed across the dirt, Jett wished he could freeze this moment, the two of them racing

together neck and neck, his mom in perfect attack position. The same as him.

And then they were at the jump!

It was a step-up, where they would leap to a higher landing. The landing would be on a tabletop, a raised stretch of flat dirt.

Jett stood tall and light as he approached the base of the jump. As he reached the face, where the ground began to curve upward, Jett dropped his body down. He pressed his feet into the pegs, keeping the bike tight against the ground. Then he hit the throttle, gunning the engine steady but strong. He rode the bike's momentum up the steep jump and into the air.

Jett felt like a seagull soaring through blue sky. He imagined that the tabletop above was the Skyline Level of the Needle, and that the little boy was pressed against a window inside, watching him. Jett sailed up and over. Then he leveled his bike and landed on the flat, high hill.

Half a second later, his mom landed beside him. She gave him a thumbs-up, and Jett soaked it all in—how the two of them had battled it out together. Even if he hadn't won, this would have been the best race ever.

"What a finish!" he heard his dad boom.

His dad and Mika were far below, at the base of

the hill. When Jett looked down at them, he almost toppled over from excitement: He suddenly knew what to do for the Needle stunt!

Jett could barely contain himself as he and his mom rode back down. As soon as they'd reached Mika and his dad, Jett took off his helmet. "I can land on the Skyline Level!"

"What are you talking about?" Mika asked.

Jett pointed to the jump that he and his mom had just done. "It'll be like a step-up tabletop," he said. "We set up a ramp, and I leap straight up. I pass the Skyline windows, then arc over the top and land on its roof!"

"Is that possible?" asked Jett's mom.

Mika took out her phone and did a quick search. She pulled up a photo of the Skyline Level. "It looks like that could work."

"Other riders have jumped onto rooftops," said Jett's dad. "How is this different?"

Jett enlarged the image on Mika's phone. It showed the ladder-like support beams of the Needle. Each had a series of wide openings along the side. "I'd leap *through* one of those openings, then arc down and land on the roof."

Jett's mom frowned. "That's quite a narrow jump space."

"I can make it," Jett said. "At least, I think I can. Mika, is it doable?"

Mika studied the image on her phone. "It will test your vertical max and maneuvering skills for sure.

But if we put a big crash pit at the bottom, it should be safe enough."

Jett grinned. "We can call it *Threading the Needle*."

His dad let loose a thunderous clap. "Crowds will flock to see that!"

"Like the World's Fair!" Jett said.

"All right, all right," said his mom. "Let's start practicing."

Jett held out a hand to Mika. "Get set . . ."

She gave him a fist bump in return. ". . . for Jett!"

CHAPTER 4

Mika's team built a setup at the practice field. They made a drop-in for Jett to pick up speed at the start. They installed a jump ramp with a steep curve. They built a platform to simulate the Skyline rooftop and put it atop an extendable crane. Then the team placed a crash pit beneath it, filled with large foam blocks.

They raised the platform twenty feet in the air.

"We'll start low," said Mika. "And work up."

Jett hopped on his bike and rode to the drop-in. He tipped his front wheel over the edge, then sped downward and raced toward the ramp. Seconds later, he swooped up and was airborne!

He was almost completely vertical, sailing straight up like it was second nature. He could never quite explain it: How he knew where and when to shift his weight. How he knew the right speed for each jump. How he could almost feel his path, a wild

but controlled arc through the air. Sometimes he wondered if he was part seagull. Mixed with flying squirrel.

Jett kept his eyes focused on the platform above. In some jumps and freestyle tricks, it was necessary to look to the side. But to thread the Needle, he would need to keep straight and narrow the whole time. Even the slightest drift of his bike could send him crashing into one of the Needle's massive support beams.

Jett cleared the front of the platform and then straightened his bike, working with gravity, not against it. He let his bike drift straight down, like a high jumper clearing a bar. Both wheels landed on the platform at the same time, and he braked to a slow stop.

"That was excellent!" Mika exclaimed in his headset.

Jett rode back to the start and practiced the twenty-foot jump over and over until he had the feel of it memorized—the exact speed, angle, and arc. Until it felt perfect.

"Now let's add the Needle opening," said Mika.

Her crew put two vertical bars on the platform. The bars were the same width apart as the opening above the Skyline Level. Then the crew added a horizontal bar to simulate the beam that Jett would have to clear before starting his downward arc onto the rooftop.

"Ready?" Mika asked.

"Always," said Jett.

He rode off the drop-in just as he had done dozens of times before. Next he increased the throttle exactly as he had done before. Then he shot up the ramp and sailed skyward.

At the horizontal bar, Jett gave the handlebars a tug to help lift the bike over. He was dead center between the vertical bars—exactly where he needed to be. After he'd cleared the horizontal bar, he tilted the bike down and landed on the platform, slowing

to a controlled stop. He took a breath and exhaled

deeply, feeling the rush.

"Jett," Mika said in his headset, "that was totally

beautiful!"

That evening, Mika used her computer to show

everyone the video footage she had taken of the

practice jumps.

"Nice!" Jett's dad said. "But we'll go higher,

right?"

"Of course, Dad."

"Based on that last jump," Mika said, "I calculated

the speed and angle Jett will need for the full stunt."

She then pulled up a photo of the Space Needle and surrounding area. "We'll put the drop-in platform in this grassy spot."

Her mom nodded. "I talked to the city and got permission. They'll also let us put padding along the Skyline's rooftop."

"Great," said Mika. "We'll have the same setup as the practice field: Jett leaps up, goes through the opening, then lands on the rooftop. I added some animation, to show his exact path." She clicked the mouse, and a line traced out Jett's route for the stunt.

"Can we actually do that?" Jett asked.

"Yes. As long as you get the right speed and arc."

"No, I mean, can we actually draw some sort of line in the air, like on the screen? Maybe with a thin rope attached to my bike? Then we'd literally be threading the Needle."

"Brilliant!" said Jett's dad. "Though a rope would be tough for crowds to see."

"It would also be risky," said Mika. "It could get caught on something. And it would be unpredictable in the air, especially if it's a windy day."

"Could you modify the exhaust?" asked Jett's mom. "Make it more visible, just for the jump?"

"Sure," said Mika. "We could put a switch on

the handlebars. When Jett flipped the switch, the exhaust would become thicker. Like the trail from an airplane."

"A Jett Stream!" said Jett and his dad at the same time. They grinned at each other.

Mika smiled and shook her head at the two Ryders. "Adding that will be easy. What we need to focus on is getting the jump high enough."

The next day, Mika's team raised the platform to thirty feet.

Jett increased his speed to account for the extra ten feet, then soared from the ramp into the air.

Halfway up, a bird coasted beside him. Jett smiled. "I'm flying with the birds!"

With a jolt of panic, Jett realized he was looking right at the bird. The phrase "you go where your eyes go" flashed through his head. And he was—he'd turned his bike slightly sideways.

Jett tried to correct his mistake, but there wasn't time. He was too far off course. He rammed into the platform's side bar. He was thrown from his bike and plummeted straight down.

Jett slammed into the crash pit. His body bounced and tumbled over the chunks of foam. Finally he came to a stop, half-buried beneath them. He did a quick

check of his body. Thankfully, nothing felt broken. He wasn't feeling too much pain, other than his head ringing. And his heart beating a thousand times per second.

His mom leaped over the pit wall in one motion and was instantly beside him. Every time he wrecked, no matter how big or small, she was always the first one there.

"Are you okay?" she asked.

"I think so."

She breathed a sigh of relief. "That was a long way down."

Jett glanced at the platform above. The fall had

been terrifying. But that was only from thirty feet. The Needle jump would be over one hundred feet high.

"Grab my hand," his mom said. "I'll help you out."

Jett was about to tell her he was fine. But his heart was still racing. He let her pull him up. After he was completely out, his mom kept hold. It reminded Jett of when he was little, when she used to take his hand to walk him around the motocross races. People would tell him how lucky he was to have a mom who was such a great rider.

Normally, Jett would have pulled his hand away as soon as he was on his feet. But now, as they walked to get his bike, Jett hung on just a little longer.

"When I was your age," his mom said, "I wrecked too many times to count. I know how scary it can be. But I also know you're the best freestyle rider I've ever seen. At any age."

Jett's heartbeat had calmed. He wanted to say that he was also the freestyle rider with the best mom in the world.

"Thanks," he said.

She gave his hand a squeeze. And then they both let go at the same time.

CHAPTER 5

It was the day of the stunt. After his wreck, Jett had practiced the jump over and over until he felt completely comfortable at thirty feet. Then he did it at forty, then fifty, then all the way up to the full height of the Skyline Level. He had practiced till perfect. But now it was time for the real thing.

Jett rolled his bike toward the starting point. He was out of sight of the crowd, but he could see the Needle towering upward with its white beams rising like spires against the blue sky.

A split second later, his dad's voice sounded over

the speakers: "Welcome from near and far! Today, in the spirit of world's fairs past, the one and only Jett Ryder will jump *through* the Space Needle!"

The crowd cheered.

Jett leaped onto his bike and rode to the drop-in so that he was visible to the crowd. The cheering got even louder.

People were lined up in every direction. They crowded both sides of the track leading to the jump ramp. They thronged the base of the Needle and the surrounding buildings. Several TV crews were set up nearby. Jett's dad had even asked the city to replace the flags at the base of the Needle. The flags

flapped in the breeze with "Today's World's Fair!" in big letters.

"And now," his dad announced, "Jett Ryder will perform a spectacle of unmatched skill, speed, and stunning dexterity!"

He went on to describe the stunt while Jett rode in a slow circle atop the starting platform. He caught a glimpse of the Skyline Level. People were lined up at its windows. Drones hovered in the air beside it, ready to capture the stunt close-up on video.

Jett's nerves thrummed as loud as his bike engine. He'd successfully done the jump over and over in practice. But if he messed up today, he would fall from more than one hundred feet. Even with the huge crash pit they had set up, he wouldn't just walk away from a fall like that.

He gripped the handlebars and imagined his mom's hand there, guiding him. Suddenly he felt calmer. He felt ready.

"And now," his dad's voice boomed, "let's *Thread the Needle*! Get set . . . for Jett!"

Jett revved his engine and did his double-donut move, which he did at the start and end of every stunt. He put his right foot on the ground and spun the bike in a full circle around it, then switched to his left foot and did the same thing. The crowd went wild.

Mika's voice crackled in his earpiece. "You got this, Jett. Thrill the world."

He rode over the edge of the drop-in, and gravity pulled him down. He was like a ski jumper building up speed. Then the track leveled, and Jett gunned the throttle. Crowds streaked by on either side, but he kept his focus on the ramp ahead. "You go where your eyes go," he told himself.

Just before the ramp, he flipped the switch to release the "Jett Stream" behind him.

As he curved up the steep ramp, his bike wobbled from the speed. But he held it straight as he went higher and higher, and then—

He was airborne!

Jett was completely vertical. His tires were facing the huge beams of the Needle. It was almost like he was riding up its side.

But Jett kept his focus on the Skyline Level. He shot toward it like a rocket.

As he approached the windows, the people inside gaped at him. Jett wondered if the little boy was in there too. He hoped so.

Suddenly Jett realized he was looking *into* the windows. He was looking to the side, just like he'd done in practice. He felt the bike shift to the left.

No!

Instantly, Jett forced his gaze straight ahead at the narrow opening above the Skyline Level. That opening was the only thing that mattered now. He had to make it through.

But he wasn't centered anymore. He was off to the side!

Panic hit him. But he had to keep the bike steady. He willed himself to focus on the spot above—the square of air he had to squeeze through.

As he reached the horizontal beam, Jett pulled the bike up to clear it, just like he had in practice.

He had enough height, but he was too wide. He was going to hit the side beam for sure.

Jett pulled his elbows in as tight as he could, trying to avoid contact. But as he sailed into the opening, his arm hit the side beam.

Jett leaned forward, willing himself through. His jacket scraped along the beam, but he kept going—and made it past!

Another inch or two wide and he would have hit more than just his sleeve. Which would have knocked him sideways. And probably backward, and then down.

Jett forced himself to keep focused. He still had to stick the landing.

He used all his strength to bring the bike from vertical to a level position. He had reached the top of his jump and was curving downward. He aimed for the padded rooftop of the Skyline Level, heading lower and lower, and then *BAM!*

The bike's tires landed on the crash pads, but he was going too fast. He was going to run into the elevator shaft that ran up the middle of the Space Needle.

Jett kept the bike balanced, steadily hitting the brakes. At the last moment, he turned it sideways. He came to a slow stop against the elevator shaft, his bike leaning gently against it.

He breathed a huge sigh of relief.

Mika's voice burst into his headset. "Jett, that was amazing! The Jett Stream was perfect—it looked just like you were threading the Needle!"

Jett turned to see the smoke trail disappearing behind him in the breeze. Nearby, a seagull floated on the air. Jett thought about how he'd wanted to fly like that, to soar to dizzying heights. He knew he couldn't do it all the time, but just for a moment, he had. For that moment, he'd felt like he was on top of the world.

Jett gave the bird a small wave. "What a ride," he said.

"Totally!" Mika answered in his headset.

Below, the crowd was going crazy. Jett rode his bike to the middle of the rooftop and did his signature double-donut move, then came to a stop and looked down. People were packed as far as he could see. He imagined the World's Fair inventors and innovators, the thrill-makers who had been here long ago.

Jett gave them a tip of his helmet. "Never stay

still . . ."

FOCUS ON
THE SPACE NEEDLE

VISION OF THE FUTURE

The Space Needle was built in 1962 for the World's Fair in Seattle, Washington. More than 2.3 million people visited the fair. Nearly 20,000 people went to the top of the Needle each day. It was meant to symbolize the future, with its flying-saucer-like observation deck and its towering spire pointing to the stars. Today, it remains one of the most famous buildings in the world.

STUNNING VIEWS

When it was built, the Space Needle was the tallest building west of the Mississippi River. It is 605 feet (184 m) high. It offers breathtaking views of Seattle, Mount Rainier, the Olympic and Cascade Mountains, and Elliott Bay. Its observation deck was remodeled in 2017. Workers added 360 degrees of floor-to-ceiling clear walls. The Skyline Level, where Jett's stunt takes place, was part of the

Needle's original design. However, it was not added until 1982. The Skyline Level provides amazing views from 100 feet (30 m) up.

AN ENGINEERING MASTERPIECE

The Space Needle was completed in just 407 days. Its passenger elevators whisk guests skyward at 10 miles per hour (16 km/h). They reach the top in just 41 seconds. The Needle's unique design also helps it survive strong winds. In windy conditions, the building twists rather than bends. The twisting happens high up, where the support beams are closest together.

THAT'S AMAZING!

ROBBIE MADDISON'S LAS VEGAS ROOFTOP JUMP

It was New Year's Eve, 2008. People in Las Vegas, Nevada, were used to spectacular shows. But the city was about to see one of its most amazing shows ever. Thousands of people had gathered at the Arc de Triomphe. This building

is a recreation of the world-famous monument in Paris, France. The crowd was waiting to witness one of the greatest motocross-stunt daredevils of all time: Robbie Maddison.

The cameras were rolling, and the lights were blazing. Maddison rode his Yamaha YZ250 bike down a drop-in platform, just like the one Jett used in his Space Needle stunt. Maddison sped along a track toward a steep jump ramp. At the base of the Arc, Maddison shot up the ramp and into the air. He soared almost completely vertically. He leaped above the 96-foot-tall (29-m-tall) Arc. Then Maddison brought his bike down for a smooth, controlled landing on the building's rooftop.

The crowd went wild. Maddison had made the stunt look simple. But he had practiced the jump for months. Maddison's crew had built a practice model at a secret location in the California desert. After the jump, Maddison appeared unhurt. But he later told his crew that he may have broken his hand.

GLOSSARY

attack position
The main motocross riding position for increasing speed and approaching jumps. The rider is standing, bending forward at the waist, knees slightly bent, elbows high, and looking forward.

crash pit
A large area at the base of a motocross stunt, usually walled-in and filled with large foam chunks or blocks. It helps break a rider's fall.

donut
A move where a rider puts one foot down and spins the bike around while riding in place, creating a circle on the ground.

drop-in
A raised platform that a rider uses to drop down into a runway toward a jump. A drop-in allows the rider to pick up speed without a long starting run.

freestyle
A type of motocross event where riders compete by doing tricks and jumps.

kickstand
A metal stand at the bottom of a bike that, when extended, allows the bike to stand up on its own.

kick-started
Started an engine by stepping down on the bike's lever.

motocross
Off-road dirt bike racing, usually done on dirt tracks with jumps.

pegs
Short metal bars that extend at foot level on either side of a motocross bike, which a rider can use for support.

revved
Increased engine speed.

rooster tail
A spray of dirt that shoots from the rear tire of a bike, usually caused by quickly spinning the tire.

step-up
A motocross jump where the landing is higher than the starting point.

throttle
A twistable grip on the dirt bike's right handlebar, which can be turned to increase or decrease engine power.

two-stroke engine
A type of engine that tends to use more fuel and is louder than a four-stroke engine, but is lighter and can work upside down.

wheelie
A move where a rider lifts the front wheel of the bike off the ground while the rear wheel stays down.

whoops
A section of motocross track made up of a series of dirt bumps. When a rider goes over these bumps by just barely touching the top of each one, it is called "skimming the whoops."

ABOUT THE AUTHOR

Sean Petrie writes books for kids, including *Welders on the Job* and *Crash Corner*. He also writes poetry, usually on the spot on a 1928 Remington typewriter. His poetry books include *Typewriter Rodeo* and the Seattle-based *Listen to the Trees*. He lives in Austin, Texas.

ABOUT THE ILLUSTRATOR

Carl Pearce lives in north Wales with his wife, Ceri. When not lost in his illustration work, he enjoys watching films, reading books, and taking long walks along the beach. He graduated from the North Wales School of Art and Design as an illustrator. His first book was published on his graduation day in 2004. He has since gone on to illustrate countless books for children.